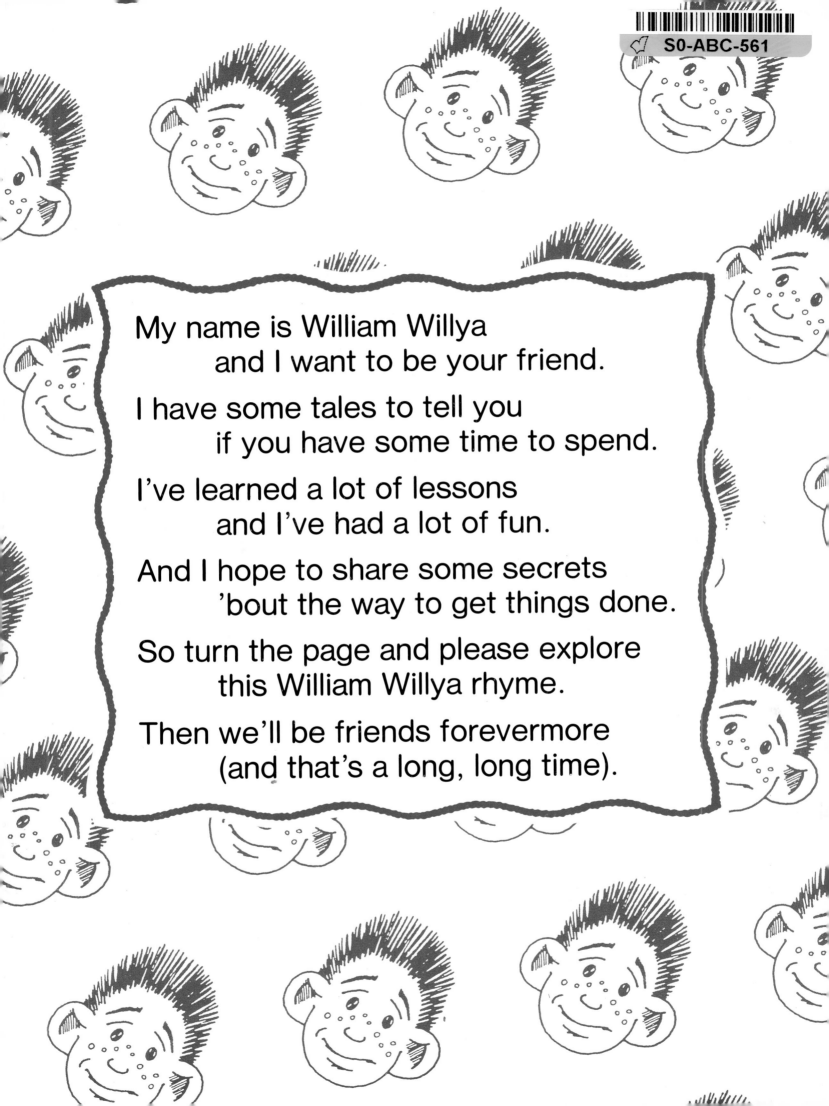

My name is William Willya
   and I want to be your friend.

I have some tales to tell you
   if you have some time to spend.

I've learned a lot of lessons
   and I've had a lot of fun.

And I hope to share some secrets
   'bout the way to get things done.

So turn the page and please explore
   this William Willya rhyme.

Then we'll be friends forevermore
   (and that's a long, long time).

William Willya®

AND THE WASHING MACHINE..

Copyright © 1993 Skip Masland

1220 Edwards Lane
Orlando, Florida 32804 USA
Phone (407) 841-5843

ISBN #1-883016-01-0

For
Haley Ann
and
Shelby Ruth…
you are my hopes,
my dreams,
my truth.

Young William Willya was ready to play

As he hopped out of bed
      on a hot summer's day.

He was planning to meet his friends
      down at the pool

Where they'd play Marco Polo
      and stay nice and cool.

As he pulled on his swimsuit
      he heard his Mom shout:

''William Willya, come down here —
      I have to go out.''

''Your sister has gone
      to a friend's house to play,

And I have to go into
      my office today.

''So before you can go to the pool,''
      she explained,

''There's a job you must do for me...''
      William exclaimed:

''But Mom! All the kids
      will be waiting for me!''

''William Willya please listen.
      It's easy,'' said she.

"There are clothes that we need
    in the washing machine,

And a second load here
    that we have to get clean.

"When the first load is finished,
    it has to be dried —

You just open the dryer and throw it inside.

"Put the second load into the washer, my dear,

And pour one cup of Spurt —
    that's the soap — right in here."

"When the first load is dry,
    simply set it aside,

Then the clothes in the washer
    will have to be dried.

"You don't have to fold them,
    I'll be home by one,

And I'm counting on you, William Willya my son.

You can go to the pool
    when the washing is done."

She showed him the buttons
for OFF and for ON,

Then she gave him a kiss,
grabbed her purse and was gone.

"What a bore!" William moaned
as he sat down to eat.

But a knock at the door
brought him straight to his feet.

"William Willya come on!" It was Molly Magoo.

"The gang is all ready —
    we're waiting for you."

"Go ahead. I can't go,"
    William said feeling blue.

"There's a couple of things
    that I still have to do."

"Things?!" exclaimed Molly.
    "Well let's get them done.

We'll just finish those things
    and then go have some fun.

We'll just get those things done
    and have fun in the sun."

"It's the wash," William said,
    "but there's not much to do.

I just have to wait 'til the first load is through,

And then while it dries I wash load
        number two.

It's just something my Mom said she needs
        me to do."

"You're in luck," Molly smiled as she yelled
        out the door:

"Go ahead! William needs me to help
        with a chore.

We'll be there in an hour — not one
        minute more!"

An hour? thought William. He wasn't
        so sure.

That Molly had given him trouble before.

"Relax William Willya," she said with a grin,
While William imagined the mess he was in.

"You really don't have to," he started to say,
But that Molly Magoo always got her own way.

"Just show me the way
        to your washing machine,
And I'll show you a trick
        to get all your clothes clean…
A trick that's as quick
        as you ever have seen."

Now William was sure this would be a mistake,

That the clothes would explode
        or the washer would break.

But maybe, just maybe, she did know a trick

That would get the wash done
        and would get it done quick.

And then, William thought, *I could go
        to the pool,*

And play Marco Polo and stay nice and cool.

"Come on William Willya," said Molly Magoo,

"If you want to go swimming,
     I know what to do."

So William showed Molly the washing machine

And she said: "This machine is
     the biggest I've seen,

And I'll bet it can get
     lots of clothes really clean."

She examined the second load
     there on the floor,

Then she turned off the washer
     and opened the door.

"This is not even full," she announced,
    "that is good.

Now I'm certain my trick
    will work just as it should.

It will work just the way that I told you it would.

"We'll put load number two
    in with load number one

And in no time at all, all the wash will be done."

William looked for himself
    and saw Molly was right.

There were just a few things
    and those things were all white —

White socks and white shirts
    and his Mother's white blouse,

And the nicest white pants
    that he had in the house.

"Come on, William Willya," said Molly Magoo,

"You can give me a hand
    loading load number two."

So they picked up those clothes:
    William's new red pajamas,

And Mother's red skirt
    with the two dancing llamas,

His sister's red dress
    and his checkerboard shirt

And a pair of red shorts
    that was covered with dirt.

Then they topped it all off
    with a cupful of Spurt.

"Now we wait, William Willya,"
    said Molly Magoo.

"When it's finished your wash
    will look better than new,

And your Mother will be so delighted with you."

So they waited

   and waited

      and waited some more

While that washing machine
        whirled away on the floor.

Then all of a sudden it stopped! It was done!

They could go to the pool!
        They could go have some fun!

They just had to put the wash in to be dried,

So they opened the door
        and they reached right inside.

"It's all pink!" William cried
        as he pulled out the clothes.

"My white pants are as pink
        as a pussycat's nose!

"And my socks and my shirts
        and my mother's white blouse!

They're as pink as the eyes
        on a little white mouse!

"You've ruined them Molly!
        Now what do we do?

I knew I should never have listened to you!"

"Hold on, William Willya. It's really not bad.
And there's really no reason for you to get mad.

"You say that these clothes
 are supposed to be white?
I don't really know,
 but suppose you are right?

"I simply don't think
 you should make such a stink,
For it's perfectly fine
 to wear clothes that are pink."

"Now I have to be going," said Molly Magoo,

"To the pool where it's cool —
        I'll be waiting for you."

And with that, Molly turned
        and she walked out the door,

Leaving William alone
        on the washing room floor.

So he sat there a minute
        and looked at the mess,

At his checkerboard shirt
        and his sister's red dress.

And then William Willya knew just what to do.

So he made a big pile and he split it in two.

He put all the reds in a pile on the right.

On the left went the pink clothes
    that used to be white.

Then he stood for a second
    and looked at the sight.

The reds were still red,
    but they had to be dried,

So he opened the dryer and threw them inside.

Then he put all the pinks
    in the wash with some Spurt,

And he hoped that the Spurt,
    which works wonders on dirt,

Would be good at removing
    the pink from a shirt.

It wasn't, of course, and the pink remained pink,

So he washed them by hand,
        one-by-one, in the sink.

And when that didn't work,
        William sat down to think.

He thought about all of his friends having fun.

He thought of his mother
        and what he had done.

If only he'd done what his mother had said.

(Or if only he'd just stayed upstairs in his bed.)

He shouldn't have listened to Molly Magoo,

But the mess he was in
        was his own fault, he knew.

When his mother came in, he was sitting inside.

The red clothes were folded.
        The pinks had been dried.

And he told her the tale
        of the washing machine,

While she stood there in silence
        and surveyed the scene.

"I know it's my fault
        and I should have known better,

But Molly took over," he sighed, "and I let her."

"You know," said his Mother,
     "I'm really not mad.

You made a mistake
     but I don't think you're bad...

And to know that you told me the truth
     makes me glad.

"Now I want you to know
     I don't mean to be cruel,

But you have to be punished
     and that means no pool,

And you'll wear these pink pants
     when you start back to school."

Then she gave him a hug
     and the clothes that were pink

And she sent him upstairs
     to his room — just to think.

So what do you think William thought
     of his mess?

Do you think he was sorry?
     The answer is yes.

But you know, William Willya will say to this day:

''If there's something to do,
     do it right.
     Then go play!''

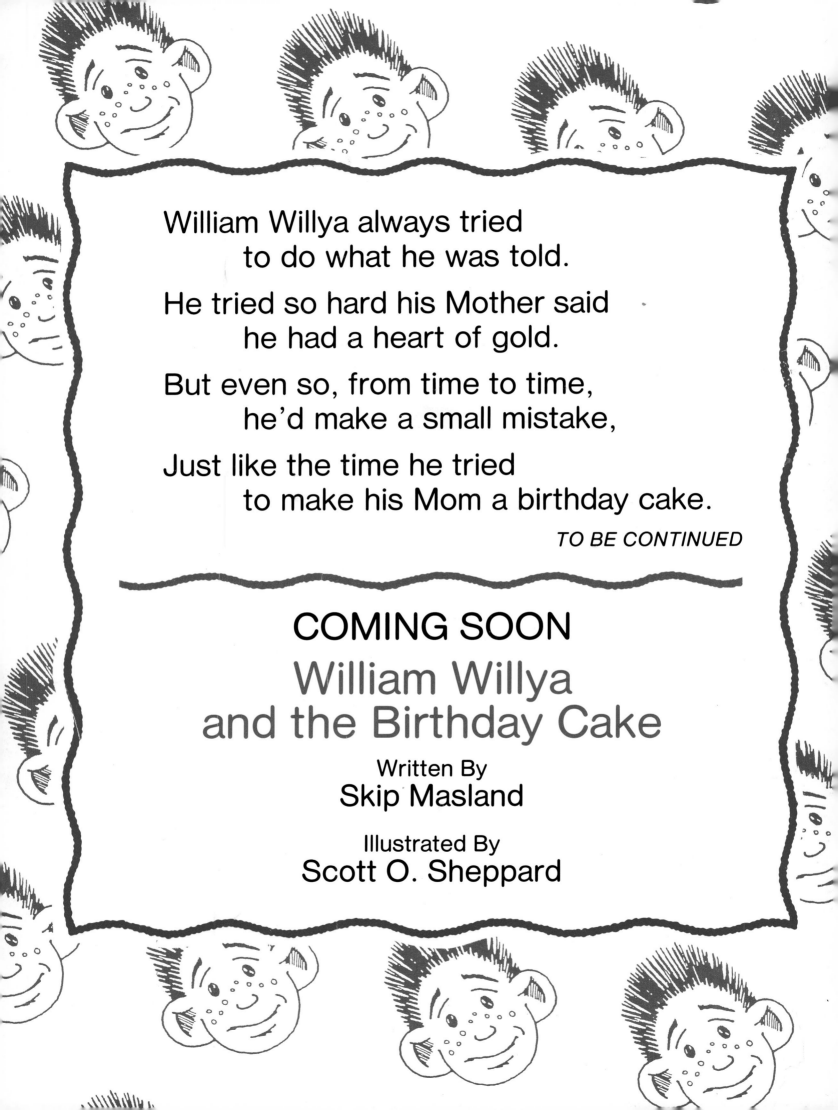

William Willya always tried
    to do what he was told.

He tried so hard his Mother said
    he had a heart of gold.

But even so, from time to time,
    he'd make a small mistake,

Just like the time he tried
    to make his Mom a birthday cake.

TO BE CONTINUED

COMING SOON

William Willya
and the Birthday Cake

Written By
Skip Masland

Illustrated By
Scott O. Sheppard